Class No. ___J___   Acc No. ___C/68485___

Author: ___WADDELL, M.___   Loc: ___/ / JUN 1997___

/ / JAN 2003

Books by the same author

MARTIN WADDELL

CUP FINAL KID

Illustrations by Jeff Cummins

WALKER BOOKS
AND SUBSIDIARIES
LONDON • BOSTON • SYDNEY

For George and Margaret Valentine –
Holmac For Ever

First published 1996 by Walker Books Ltd
87 Vauxhall Walk, London SE11 5HJ

This edition published 1997

2 4 6 8 10 9 7 5 3 1

Text © 1996 Martin Waddell
Illustrations © 1996 Jeff Cummins

This book has been typeset in Garamond.

Printed in England

British Library Cataloguing in Publication Data
A catalogue record for this book
is available from the British Library.

ISBN 0-7445-5240-0

CONTENTS

HERBIE'S BIG CHANCE

One Friday Herbie Bazooka was sitting in his mum's kitchen guzzling a cheeseburger when the F.A. Cup Final Preview came up on TV.

It was Wombledon Town versus Hottenham Totspur. The man on TV said Totspurs would get stuffed, because their star striker was injured and out of the game.

Herbie gulped down his burger,
grabbed his Totspur supporter's
scarf and hat and set off for the
ground, running as fast as he could.

Herbie hopped over the stadium wall and ran out on to the pitch. Although he looked small and fat he was super-fit. But…

Herbie was about one metre high, which means he was small for his age. He also wore crummy old glasses. Herbie didn't look much like a footballer, but looks aren't everything. Herbie Bazooka knew he was a star!

"Because you're a skill-team, and my grandfather Julio played for Brazil!" Herbie announced.

Coach was impressed, because you have to be good to play for Brazil. "OK!" grinned Coach. "Get changed, kid. We'll give you a trial!"

HERBIE MAKES THE TEAM!

I'm not just a small, fat kid with glasses! I'm Herbie Bazooka and I play in the park with my dad every Sunday!

Herbie changed into some kit that they brought him, though the shirt and the shorts were too big. They made Herbie look daft.

"I'll show you!" Herbie cried, and set to work with his football.

Herbie
back
flicked.

Herbie
ball
juggled.

Herbie cannonball shot with his right, then with his left … breaking the net.

Herbie hit corner-inswingers and outswingers.

The team were amazed. They'd never seen anyone play like Herbie Bazooka, except maybe Pelé.

"That's how the game's played in Brazil!" gasped Coach. And Herbie was picked for the Cup Final team as their mystery striker.

"This game will make me a star!" cried Herbie Bazooka.

That night Herbie Bazooka
appeared on "Top of the Pops"
with the Hottenham team. They
sang the team's Cup Final song…

21

It went on for a bit like that. It was
a rotten song and it wasn't true,
because none of them really did play
like Brazil, except Herbie Bazooka.

Everyone was impressed by the little
kid in the front row who was
snapping his fingers and rapping
like mad, in between verses.

"That kid could be Golden-disc *big!*" the "Top of the Pops" man said. He told the little kid he could have any money he wanted if he would sign up as a pop singer and go on TV every week.

"Don't sign!" cried the rest of the team. "The kid's in our team. He's our mystery striker!"

"He can't be!" said the man. "He's small, fat and eight!"

"But he plays like they play in Brazil," said the team.

The TV man laughed. He didn't believe it.

"Just wait till you see me at Wembley's twin towers!" cried Herbie Bazooka.

HERBIE AT WEMBLEY
FIRST HALF

Coach had put Herbie out on the wing with instructions to roam everywhere and not to get hurt, and to score wonder-goals like they score in Brazil. Herbie tried hard, for he knew it was tough at the top. He ran straight down the middle.

He ran up for the first long ball.

Herbie cut in from the wing.

The ball went in touch. So did Herbie Bazooka, flat on his face. The Wombledon players were grinning and laughing. They'd sorted out Totspurs' mystery striker. Totspurs were struggling to get into the game.

So that's what Herbie did.

Now Herbie was brilliant. Herbie saved Totspurs again and again!

Then someone bashed little Herbie and knocked off his glasses.

Herbie was down on his knees, as Wombledon's star striker volleyed for goal…

Everyone cheered. No one knew how Herbie got back. The last anyone knew, he'd been down on his knees finding his glasses, which just shows how fast Herbie could go! But then…

SMASH!

Herbie's glasses were broken!
That put Herbie in trouble!
Coach moaned and groaned.

Wombledon Town got right on top.

Totspurs looked beaten, but then Herbie at last saw the ball, coming at him out of the haze. Herbie brought it down on to his chest.

He jinked and he turned and he went past one man and another, then twisted inside, and lashed in a shot from the edge of the box, just like they do in Brazil!

Nobody on his team cheered, because Herbie had run the wrong way, which was easy to do when you've busted your glasses. It was the Worst-ever Wembley Own Goal put in his own net by Herbie Bazooka!

WOMBLEDON TOWN 3
HOTTENHAM TOTSPURS 0

It looked as if Herbie was finished.

F.A. CUP FINAL SECOND HALF

Coach still had faith in what Herbie could do. He sent out for a very strong glue and stuck Herbie's glasses together again.

"You're in the team because you play like they play in Brazil!" Coach told Herbie. "So go out and do it for me!"

The teams lined up to kick off, and Herbie Bazooka put the ball down on the centre-spot. Then Herbie looked round.

The Wombledon goalie was out at
the edge of the penalty area, tying
his boots. He hadn't touched the ball
once in the first half and he wasn't
expecting to touch it in the second
half either. Herbie spotted the
chance. He took a long run up and…

Herbie had scored direct from the kick-off! And there were still forty-four minutes and fifty-nine seconds to go!

**WOMBLEDON TOWN 3
HOTTENHAM TOTSPURS 1**

The crowd roared.

And that's just what Totspurs did!

But … all the long balls were up
in the air, and Herbie Bazooka was
tiny, as ace strikers go.

The stopper headed every ball
back, and each time he landed on …
Herbie Bazooka!

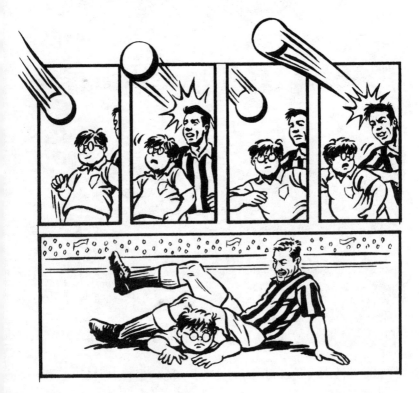

Herbie talked to his widemen. "Keep playing long balls!" he ordered. "But not long balls direct on their stopper's head. I want it so he has to run backwards to head out, then I can cut across him from behind."

That's what they did. Three times they tried it, and three times Herbie was blocked by the stopper, but the fourth time…

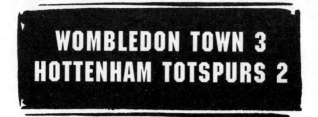

**WOMBLEDON TOWN 3
HOTTENHAM TOTSPURS 2**

A great header from Herbie Bazooka! You don't have to be big to score goals in the air, just move in from behind and time your jump well, and height can be made not to matter.

Twenty minutes to go!

Wombledon knew just what
Herbie could do now, and that's
why they set out to get Herbie.

Herbie was brought down from
behind on the edge of the box.

Herbie did just what they do in
Brazil! It was a Bazooka banana
inside the far post.

WOMBLEDON TOWN 3
HOTTENHAM TOTSPURS 3

Ten minutes to go, and a hat trick
from Herbie Bazooka! But…

"Oh no!" cried the fans. Herbie looked hurt and was limping about on the wing.

"Come off, Herbie!" cried Coach. "I'll send the sub on." But Herbie just winked and stayed put.

That's clever, Herbie! That's a trick they play in Brazil!

Five minutes to go!

Suddenly ... very slow, badly hurt Herbie Bazooka –

became rocket-paced Herbie,
not hurt at all!

Herbie nut-megged the keeper,
just like they do in Brazil!

Herbie Bazooka was Man of the
Match! He got the Cup and his

Cup Winner's Medal and went on
TV and was famous that night.

On Sunday Herbie spent all day in bed nursing his bruises but on Monday he went back to school, riding on top of a bus with his team and the Cup … just like they do in Brazil!

MORE WALKER SPRINTERS
For You to Enjoy